I0645918

BEYOND
THE
BOUNDARIES

ALAEZI DIKE

Copyright © 2021 Alaezi Dike

All rights reserved. No part of this publication may be reproduced,
distributed, or transmitted in any form or by any means, including
photocopying, recording, or other electronic or mechanical methods,
without the prior written permission of the author or publisher, except
in the case of brief quotations embodied in critical reviews and certain
other noncommercial uses permitted by copyright law.
For permission requests, email the author: Alaezidike222@gmail.com

ISBN: 978-0-983970-3-2 | Paperback ($19.95)
ISBN: 978-0-9893970-9-4 | Hardcover ($24.95)
ISBN: 978-0-983970-4-9 | e-Book ($4.99)

Any references to historical events, real people, or real places are used
fictitiously. Names, characters, settings and places are creative
reflections of the author's imagination.

Book Editing & Front cover design by Chido Nwangwu
Book inside design by

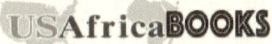

Houston | New York | Washington DC | London | Lagos | Johannesburg

Produced by USAfrica International, in the United States of America.

First print edition 2021.

Books@USAfricaBooks.com
USAfricaBooks@gmail.com
USAfricaBooks.com
Phone: +1-832-45-CHIDO (24436)

DEDICATION

To the memory of my parents, Elder H. W. Ajunwa
and Elder (Mrs) L. N. Ajunwa. Especially, for
consistently providing the same educational
opportunities and access to girls and boys!

MY STORY

I n this novel, I tell the engaging story of a very determined girl's tumultuous but fateful past which began during the Nigeria-Biafra war (1967 - 1970) until....

It's set in the context of the realities of the impact of war especially on girls, young women and families around the environment where I grew up in the southeastern Nigeria, and connects to the northerly middle-belt of Nigeria. For many individuals in other environments around the world, there will be familiar lessons.

FOREWORD

Alaezi Dike's "Beyond the Boundaries" is a fictionalized story based-on-true-events. Her rendering is done with such incredible attention to detail that those who experienced the Nigeria-Biafra war of 1967 to 1970 will attest to the authenticity and its author.

The full range of human experience is so masterfully explored, that many persons reading it will see themselves in the story.

The heroine of the story exudes a moral aptitude and adaptability that will inspire readers and give testament to the inconvenient truths of how war impacts women and girls.

I was curious, for three reasons, when I first picked up this book/novel. First, my family and I lived through the Nigeria - Biafra war of 1967 to 1970.

Second, to this day, I remember those deadly "air raids" and fleeing our home the night before Christmas of 1969, shortly before the war ended.

Third, would reading finely and realistically woven story resurrect past trauma, create new memories, or simply be a detached ("human-less"?) retelling of an ugly period in Nigeria's post-colonial history?

With these questions, I began to read…, and what I found was an extraordinary rendering of one young woman's experience of the true realities of the war.

It's a story not only deserving to be told, but needing to be read and witnessed by all who come in contact with it. Or those who were impacted by the events of the time.

No one else could have done this better than Alaezi Dike (nee Ajunwa) whom I have known since our time together in high school, in the 1970s.

Her resilience, intelligence and willingness to explore events that many of us would rather forget are evident on the forthcoming pages. Being the courageous writer she is, the author has created a work that will haunt and inspire those who want to ensure that war does not happen again.

Evidently, Alaezi's creativity, courage and wisdom brought this engaging story to light. May we all be changed by it.

Dr. Lilian I. Asomugha
Los Angeles, USA

ACKNOWLEDGEMENT

First, I appreciate my amazing husband, Dr. Chima Dike, an Elder of the Presbyterian Church of Nigeria. He read the first draft of the novel and encouraged me to continue and conclude the story.

I'm grateful to Dr. Lillian Asomugha who took time to read the novel, provided suggestions and encouraged me to present it for publication.

I thank the phenomenal editor and publisher, Dr. Chido Nwangwu. I appreciate your motivation, editing insights and facts-driven pointers to actual dates of events and correct names of major players of that war.

My sincere thanks goes to the following individuals that had a sneak preview of the novel and made an impact: Prof. Okoro Kanu Ijoma, Prof. Clement Anyiwo, Mazi Kanu Ivi and Mazi Enyi Kanu.

I would like to thank my children:
Dr. Nnamdi Dike
Dr. Ezenwa Dike
Dr. Obianuju Erinma Felix
Chinenyugo Amaka Nnodu
Okeigbo Chima Dike
Eng. Uzodinma Dike

To my grandchildren:
Chinonso Uddy Felix
Adugo Breanna Dike
Ezinne Urechi Felix
Isioma Bridget Dike
Chidera Mirielle Nnodu
Adaora Brielle Dike
Benjamin Obinna Dike
Brooklyn Chinaza Dike
Akachi Asher Dike
Chimadike Felix

I extend special thanks to my siblings:
Prof. Dr. Margaret Ijeoma Aguwa
Mazi Uche O. Ajunwa
Eng. Chima Ajunwa
Attorney Grace Ogo Ajunwa
Dr. Peace Nnennaya Jessa

And, to our wider family for their consistent support and prayers.

Alaezi Dike
June 13, 2021
Dallas, Texas

1
THE
KIDNAP

I t's the early hours of the dry season in the South Eastern Nigeria community of Atani village in Arochukwu. The historic community is only a few miles from the ocean tributary called the Bight of Biafra, at the time. It had been so named, many decades before the 1967 declaration of the Republic of Biafra.

As Atani awakens, one can hear the buzzing of crickets feeding on the grass and bees pollinating the flowers.

On this day, we set forth to the udara tree to collect its fruits (the African Star apple).. Udara is a popular fruit in West Africa. This sweet and sour fruit has some wonderful health benefits such as the prevention of mouth gum disease, tackling of toothache and sore throat. The milky juice that comes out of it when squeezed or sucked is not only satisfying like the chewable back but also helps with constipation and indigestion. This fruit is known as 'agbalumo' by the Yorubas and called 'chiwo' by the Hausas.

Its herbal, medicinal values are known in many West African countries such in Republic of Benin, Togo and Ghana. It is often used to treat ailments such as malaria and yellow fever. Both the fruit and its kernel are edible.

The demand for this useful fruit is very high, hence my cousin, Ngozi, and I made it a point to get to the tree earlier than others. We leave the house before the first cock crow; around 4.00 am. We sell them to the early traders who go to the nearby neighboring markets.

Due to the location of Arochukwu, we enjoy the privilege of attending our own market, which is mainly on nkwo market days, and the daily market at Obinkita village.There are other nearby markets in Ututu, the Afoebi market. They have their market days on Afor days, Ihechiowa has the Ahia Nworie, on Orie market days. Atani Aniyom market on Eke days. There was the option of going to Nmaku market on some Afor market days.

Nmaku is a neighboring Ibibio town, approximately 10 (kilometers).

For individuals from the middle class to upper class families, they go to these markets to buy than to sell, but for the individuals like us from poor homes we go there mostly to sell our garri, fufu, vegetables, maize, okro and fruits depending on the season and sometimes to purchase other products.

On getting to the tree we were excited to see that there were many fruits on the ground.

Ngozi and I were the first to get there and we felt lucky as we were picking and filling our baskets with excitement. Barely 8 minutes, Ngozi screamed. I quickly turned but she was pointing to something, someone behind me.

Before I could turn around, two brawny, masculine hands grabbed me and lifted me, effortlessly. I scuffled to extricate myself from the clasp but every effort I made proved abortive as the assailant tightened his grip and covered my mouth. He stopped me from shouting. I could hear him tell his partner in crime "Leave that one; she's too young!"

My cousin's frightened scream of "ewhoooo!" tore through the serene break of dawn....
She ran for safety, away, while my captor and his cohort hurried into the nearby forest. He held me tightly and firmly on his broad shoulders. He clinched harder as I tried to get him to let go of me. Inside the forest (ude), I could hear the howling of the grey eagle owl.
I could not see the face of the other person, but my assailant kept instructing him on the direction.

Amidst all those, I wondered if my fragile cousin will be able to get home safely and get help to look for me. My thought was interrupted when my kidnapper said, 'Let's rest for a while". He also asked to know if anybody was following. The other man responded "No ".

One of the men removed the scarf from my face and warned me to keep quiet.

I noticed the familiar big Tertulia Africana tree, which is called ukwa (Breadfruit). It looked familiar, even in the darkness, I immediately suspected that this breadfruit tree is one of those near Mazi Odimegwu's farm. Every son or daughter of the village knew his farm. I started mapping out possible ways to escape when and if an opportunity presented itself.

At this point, the other man brought out a dark scarf and covered my eyes and threatened that if I shout or cry out, they will kill me. My entire body trembled with fear.

I began to plead but was told that it will worsen my situation. I pleaded that "I'm an orphan" — hoping that this will draw sympathy for me. I was warned never to speak and to only speak when I am asked.

Why did these strange men who spoke broken English with an accent set upon us, without any of our strong warriors seeing or stopping them?

After all, we are grandsons and daughters of the great Arochukwu warriors and heroes.

After about five minutes of resting, the other man encouraged the one that abducted me to start walking. They untied my legs; kept my hands tied and asked me to walk as fast as I can. The two men were on both sides of me and we followed a narrow winding path, until we got to a nearby river.

They decided to move further to an area that was less steep. We must have walked about two hours. I saw some villagers fetching water from the stream.

I was warned not to talk to anyone.

They now changed from speaking broken English to the local

language, which was Ibibio.

We passed different groups of farmers and villagers, we walked through the bush for almost 75 minutes. One of them stayed with me, while the other went to get food and water but before he left, he warned the other to make sure that he does not do anything to harm me.

He also reminded him that the military generals pay more for virgins. That was when I figured out why I was kidnapped....

Early that morning, in Atani, my cousin was crying to my aunt Nwaka and her husband Mazi Ogwo, about my capture.

But to them it seemed an unbelievable story. Auntie Nwaka's husband encouraged our auntie not to worry that he will go with Ngozi to check out my story.

When Ngozi and Mazi Ogwo got to the location of the udara tree, there were about five persons there. They were asked if they could corroborate Ngozi's story. Only two persons confirmed they saw her running back to the village shouting hysterically without knowing why. They did not witness the kidnapping.

Mazi Ogwo reported the matter to the village head, Eze Ogo Igboko, and to Mazi Onuoha, the Headmaster. Mazi Onuoha normally represents the village with the Biafran soldiers on matters of security. He was able to get the military to work with the local young men to join to quickly set up a search party for me, Ijego. The village had very few young men, as they had all joined the Biafran army, navy or air force.

Mazi Onuoha however met with the village head to arrange for some middle-aged men to work with a handful of military policemen to comb the surrounding neighborhood bushes....

The next morning, Uncle Ogwo interrogated Ngozi further, as he did not want to make a fool of himself in front of the Eze.

On their way home, he threatened her to stop telling tales and that he believed that "Ijego decided to run away and will come back when she decides to come home."

Ngozi could not believe it, as she witnessed how Ijego was snatched.. She muttered to herself "Ije Ije, how can I help you? Who do I tell? What do those men want to do with you?"

All day, Ngozi prayed silently to God almighty to guide and direct Ije. Since Ngozi and Ijego lost their mothers, their Aunt Nwaka was kind enough to take them in and support them. Although her husband, Mazi Ogwo, did not like the idea, Aunty Nwaka worked hard to support them to the best of her ability. She provided motherly care to them.

Ngozi decided to talk to her aunt, later that day when she gets back from selling agidi — which she usually carried to different places and will not come home, until she sold the entire batch for the day.

She later spent time telling Auntie Nwaka the details of what transpired during the kidnaping of her cousin Ije.

The next morning, when Ijego did not return home, the middle-aged warriors and some volunteers as well as two military policemen were sent to the nearby bushes to look for her. They spent 5 days combing the bushes and farmlands looking but without success. The villagers were disappointed how such heinous crime could happen in their community without a trace.

Ijego's village, Atani nmawuru of Arochukwu is one of the nineteen (19) villages in Arochukwu. Arochukwu people of the Eastern Nigerian are an Igbo sub-group that was, for some time, part of the Calabar/Ibibio administrative province.

Historically, the present day Arochukwu town is the third largest in Abia State. Atani shared common boundaries with the Ibibios at the time, and still do in the present day Akwa Ibom State. Atani village is bordered by other Arochukwu villages such as Isinkpu, Asaga, Amuvi and Amukwa.

Using the bush path, the village is flanked by Obinkita, Amuvi, and Asaga and at the verge after the farmlands are Akwa Ibom villages. The earlier inhabitants of the village were made up of celebrated warriors from different other Arochukwu villages.

They were strategically selected to live in Atani as strong men and women to assist in notifying the other Arochukwu villages, when an enemy is encroaching and if possible, fight to chase them off before other warriors can join them. They use the ikoro (a big wooden instrument) that can be heard from Atani to other villages to notify the others of any impending danger.

This role was carefully handled and executed at that time with the warriors fighting the enemies and pushing them far beyond the river. These fearless warriors of audacity became successful, rich farmers, traders and eventually their children and grandchildren became teachers', educators and businessmen. These villagers themselves, with a sense of pride based on this history, believe that no mortal can take advantage of them and get away with it.

After many days of searching for Ijego, the community members encouraged her family to seek the advice of a traditional, native doctor. The native doctor, Mazi Ajah told them: "yes, she is in captive in a strange land, however she will eventually come home....."

The case was eventually reported to the local Biafra Military police, but nothing came out of it. Discouraged, downhearted and heartbroken, her family decided to hand over everything to God, believing that one day they will see her alive — as the native doctor "predicted."

2
FROM UNCOMPLETED BUILDING TO MILITARY CAMP

The next day, we walked all day until my legs could no longer carry me. After several miles, one of the men would get some fruits and water for us to eat and drink.

Each time we stopped, they will talk in their local Anang or Ibibio language. One of the key words I kept hearing from them was akamando otto.

Not knowing what it means, I assumed that the word had something to do with me. Each time they said it, they looked at me, then at each other and they both end up with a broad, mischievous smile. Each time they do this, I will pray to God to protect me from these evil men. Rev. Sister Mary thought us in our Sunday school, that we will always have evil men and women around us and that we should pray against such people. In my heart, I kept praying, even as we walked inside the thick forest, until we suddenly stopped a little further from an uncompleted building.

The elderly, stronger looking man, my kidnapper, told the second man to go and check out the place while we hide in a nearby bush. When he came back, he nodded for us to proceed.

The surrounding of the house had weeds all over the place and graffiti's obviously made by hoodlums on the walls of the building. The air of fear and loneliness the atmosphere evoked made it a perfect location for a horror movies.

Entering the uncompleted building from the bush, the surroundings of the building were dotted with heaps of smelly wastes. I was taken through one of the back doors to a room with an old mattress and a dirty bed sheet. The thought that kidnappers, ritualists, armed robbers and cultists will find this kind of building useful for their nefarious activities, immediately crossed my mind. I knew that it's not a safe place for a young twelve-year-old like me to be with two villains. I noted that such a location will attract animals and scavengers who go to the trash heaps daily to collect discarded items. I prayed that I will have an opportunity to meet someone who will help me out. On second thoughts, I realized that this is a place to hide where people leave early in the morning to stow away.

Unknown to me I had crossed the enemy line, and the persistent air raid my village had suffered from the Nigerian enemy troops, may not happen in these parts. It was wishful thinking. We witnessed in the last two years a lot of bombings by air raids and jet fighters that members of these communities hide in the bushes during the day. My thought was interrupted by the question: who is the enemy now?
I wondered, was it the men that violently took me from my village or the Nigerian soldiers who violently kill innocent Biafrans?

I kept praying silently for the Lord that sister Mary had told us about, to come down from heaven to save me. Tired from travel fatigue I was burnt out and must have dozed off when I was suddenly awakened by the shake from the stronger man.

This time his face was not covered. He was skinny but strong with pimples on his face, approximately 5'8". His clothes looked tattered and his boots had small tinny holes. His face was oblong, hardened, and bold. I immediately knew that a proud and audacious face like this will never be kind to me. His meanness exudes even in his nonverbal reaction and looks. He brought a towel and soap and dropped them on the bed and asked me to pick them up and follow him. I was led to the back yard to a makeshift bathroom, where water, soap was kept and directed me to clean up myself. A new, clean and oversized outfit was given to me to wear in the meantime.

By the time I came out of the bathroom, I noticed that a plate of egwusi soup and garri were placed on the makeshift table. I was instructed to eat the food. As I was very hungry, I hurriedly ate the food, without thinking about contamination. I gulped down the water that was put in a dirty plastic cup with stains. I promised myself that I need to be strong to survive.

Not long after, I heard this strong, nearby shelling and firing. It was so close as if it was next block.

At this time, two men in unique military uniform entered the uncompleted building from the back. This military uniform was different from the Biafra Military uniform. It was at this time that it dawned on me that I had been kidnapped by "the real enemy", the Nigerian soldiers and what I will do going forward will depend on how I control the situation.

They also gave me a smaller uniform size military uniform for me to wear and follow them without looking back. I was also warned that if I stand and raise my head that I am likely to die and that if I lay low and obey the rules that I will survive.

One of the men threw a bag to my attacker who thanked him and looked excited. My attacker turned, looked at me with disgust and said to the men in the uniform "Nice doing business with you. We will be back next market day, please look for us."

He disappeared through the back door. I chose to obey and live, instead of disobeying and die. We exited the building from the side and headed to a path area that eventually led to a river. When we got to the shallow end of a river, I was warned not to say a word and that if I say anything or shout, I could be killed. I nodded my head in affirmation. Immediately after we crossed the river, we emerged in an environment that looked like an abandoned school compound and I was taken to a big room where I saw other girls and young women on mats, on the floor. A mat was given to me and I was asked to take it to one side and lay on the floor like others. Another younger man came and put handcuff on my hand just like the others. I noticed all the girls and women in the room were all handcuffed like me.

I lay on the mat praying for a while and crying quietly, not knowing what will become of me. After a while, some well-dressed military men came in. I noticed them pointing to select the women and girls of their choices. I turned my eyes down to the mat, refusing to make an eye contact with any of them, until one elderly man instructed the men to untie me.

He took me outside and took me to a clean army vehicle, unlike the ones I had seen in the last two years of Biafra Military vehicles. He drove off and asked me in broken English," wetin be your name" I was petrified to speak, he immediately asked "how old you be ". I said twelve, in a small voice. He immediately said. "Sorry my daughter, na my job I de do, I will send you to a better man, If I no do am, I go get into trouble ".

I was not exactly sure what he was talking about, but his voice was sympathetic, fatherly and kind. He quickly turned the car around and headed to the other direction. When he stopped, he left me in the car and knocked on the door, a younger and cleaner shaven officer came out and they spoke. I heard him say, "Oga, I brought this pikin to you because I know you be good man. I was asked to deliver her to Oga Major Johnson, but I know he go maltreat am, so I decided to bring her to you. Oga I beg you take care of her. She be small girl."

The other man said to him "okay Akpan, thank you; please manage it so that you will not get into trouble with the Major, you know how he is and what he is capable of doing to you or me, if he knows what you did".

I immediately noted the face and the name of this kind, elderly Akpan who felt sorry for me. I was asked to get out of the car into an apartment, which has a small but well-furnished comfortable living room. Inside the apartment, the younger man he spoke with asked me to "sit down and get some rest first."

The younger man introduced himself as James Banfa, of the 82nd Brigade of the Nigerian Army. He asked me if I was hungry and he brought me water to drink. He instructed another person to bring me some food. As I swigged on the cup of water, he looked directly at me and asked me. "Please tell me about yourself and how old are you "? He was very well spoken, and his English was different from what I am used to. He spoke with a fluent accent and sounded more like that of then Col. Yakubu Gowon, the Head of State and Commander in Chief of the Nigerian Armed forces—which we hear on the radio.

I was afraid and unsure of what to tell him as I introduced myself.
He immediately said "You are an Igbo girl."
I nodded in affirmation.
"How did you get here?" he asked?
"I was kidnapped from my home village by two unknown men and I ended up here" I responded.
"Where am I?"

He said "This is Ikono and I am a soldier from the northern Nigeria, deployed in the place to fight against the Biafran solders and their supporters. And, here I am with a very young girl who is like a little sister. What these men are doing in this camp is wrong. We were given a clear mandate not to touch nor harm children and women, but these worthless untrained soldiers have converted this camp into a camp of rape and sexual aggression". Before he could finish his sentence I tried to image what he was trying to express to me, hence,

I started sobbing and he encouraged me to stop crying and immediately told me he will do everything possible to help me. My crying got to him and I could hear him speaking out of the corner of his mouth, that he did not sign up in the army to molest and rape innocent girls and that what is going on at the camp where innocent girls and women are held against their will is indecent and not acceptable and hence should be reported to the authorities.

He asked if I wanted to bath, clean up first, before eating. I opted to clean myself up first and he showed me to a small bathroom with soap and clean bath towels. While in the bathroom, I cried and prayed to God to take authority and control of my life.

After eating the bowl of rice placed on the table for me, I had my bath. Shortly, I slept off on the bed in the room.

3
WAR
AND
GIRLS

My first few week in Ikono was full of learning experiences. Officer James Banfa, I quickly learned, was a Captain in the Nigerian Army from the Christian section of Plateau State.

He sent Mr. Akpan to purchase clothing of my size and had instructed the cook to allow me cook food of my choice. From time to time, he allowed me to also relate with a few of the girls who are attached to the officers. I was instructed not to mix up too much however I did more of listening than talking. Captain James made it clear that I should not discuss my unique situation with him with others.

I learnt that women and girls are abducted from near and faraway places, particularly the Biafra areas, for the purposes of supplying Nigerian soldiers' sexual pleasures....

I also discovered that men who handle the procurement and kidnapping are heavily rewarded, especially when they supply underage girls like me who are categorized as virgins.

More often the victims they kidnap for sexual slavery are young girls and younger women and in many cases their victimization comes under the terms of military duty.

I also understand that sometimes some of the girls and young women, especially those who are not attached to a person assist in collecting firewood and in carrying weapons. Girls not attached to an officer are shared to different soldiers and officers as sex slaves.

They are kept in the abandoned school dormitories. Many are forced to satisfy about a dozen military men per night. Many of them get pregnant and their babies are taken away from them and taken to the local orphanage. These babies are eventually given out to Army officer who are looking for children, who will send these children away to their various homes.

Unknown to me some of the officers were not happy that Captain James Banfa "kept me to himself" and kept teasing him about keeping only me, not sharing me and not wanting to partake in "screwing" the other girls.

It was tough learning the differential impact of armed conflict and the specific vulnerabilities of girls and women.

During conflict flights, women and girls remain at high risk for sexual violence committed by bandits, insurgency groups, military and border guards.

Many girls and women flee war zones without the added safeguard of male relatives or community members, further increasing their vulnerabilities of falling into wrong hands.

I spent countless hours listening to stories about the physical injuries, such as bruises, stabbings, and fractures and psychological abuses the girls go through, whenever they refuse to fall in line. Scaring stories of what other young girls in the camp had experienced, such as vaginal tearing, bleeding, infection, or chronic pelvic pain.

In extremely brutal cases, the physical harm of rape can lead to the girl developing different diseases and sexually transmitted diseases. As a result of the consistent abuse of a young girls who are still not fully developed to experience sexual intercourse a few ended up having an abnormal disease called Vaginal Fistula, an opening that connects the Vagina to another organs, such as your bladder, colon or rectum can be created. This abnormal connection or passageway that connects two organs or vessels that do not usually connect can develop anywhere between an intestine and the skin, between the vagina and the rectum, and other places, between the anus, or between the vagina and the bladder. Girls with vaginal fistula tend to be incontinent, isolated, and stigmatized.

I was told by one of the ladies who has been there longer than others that a few of the girls diagnosed from the camp of having vaginal fistula were taken out from the camp at the middle of the night. Rumor has it that they were shot and buried in unknown locations, instead of getting medical care for them. This is an ailment that is most often treated with surgery to remove the damaged part of the body. Because it was war period they did not care for the lives of the girls and to avoid problems they destroyed innocent lives. After hearing these stories, I prayed to God to be with me, to avoid issues like this and to still have the courage to stay and to survive.

I was worried about my Auntie Nwaka, her two little children Uzoma and Ihedi, my cousin Ngozi and my grandfather Pa Ugochukwu. Uncle Ogwo, Auntie Ngozi's husband has never liked the fact that she took us in after we became orphans. If they are all alive, I suspect he will be happy that one of us is gone and will think that it is good as he will have one less mouth to feed. Not sure of whether they were dead nor alive, I prayed to God that they are all alive so that, we can reconnect when the war ends. I was convinced that I can hide under the protection of Captain James Banfa until when the war will end.

Sometimes I spend time thinking of what has happened to me within a short time of my life. It was just like yesterday that the war started, and I was a happy kid, looking forward to attending school since I did well in my standard six class. Aunty Nwaka did not have any other formal education after her primary education. Her parents did not appreciate the importance of sending a girl child to secondary school. She is a hard-working woman who did not have opportunity to go to school.

She had committed to sending me, cousin Ngozi and her daughter Ihedi to secondary school to avoid early marriage and to acquaint us with useful skills that will be valuable in future. Unfortunately, the Muslim Hausas in northern Nigeria began massacring the Christian Igbos who were living in their region, prompting tens of thousands of Igbos to flee to the East, where their people were the dominant ethnic group.

My understanding as a young twelve year old girl was that the Igbos doubted that Nigeria's oppressive military government would allow them to develop, or even survive, so on May 30, 1967, the then Military Administrator of the South Eastern Region, Lieutenant Colonel Odumegwu Ojukwu and other non-Igbo representatives of the area established the Republic of Biafra, comprising several states of Nigeria. Five weeks after its secession from Nigeria, the breakaway Republic of Biafra is attacked by Nigerian government forces, hence, war between Nigeria and Biafra broke out in July 1967. Biafra had to defend themselves. The Biafra army made some initial advances, but Nigeria's superior military strength gradually reduced Biafra territory. Border Towns such as Eha Amufu, Nsukka, Ninth Mile, Enugu, Port Harcourt, Bonny, Calabar, and Onitsha were all blocked by the Nigerian troops.

The blockade against Biafra made essential commodities scarce, forcing women to make the treacherous days journey behind enemy lines on foot to go to "Ahia attack ", market behind the enemy lines. At a time, the remaining of Biafra was divided into Biafra 1 and 2. Traders were moving from one side of Biafra to the other side, across the enemy line.

Many elderly people and children were sick, bloated, extremely pale in color, their hair turned white and curly. The women traders worked hard to help their families to keep them alive. They bought looted property from both Nigerian and Biafran soldiers, as well as salt, dried milk and egg, stock fish, cigarettes, potash, salt, and marijuana and other items. These "Ahia attack" women traders on the trail sometimes were raped and killed by soldiers on both sides, while others die in bombing raids or improvised explosive devices or land mine placed to prevent enemy cross over. I knew about the "Ahia attack" before I was kidnaped, but nothing in my wildest imaginations would prepare me for what happened to me and the stories I heard from other captured girls and women.

Unknown to many, some lazy men who refused to go to war were busy trafficking on women and young girls, servicing soldiers on both sides of the river. I heard this from the other captured girls and women and that exposed me to this dangerous phenomenon and to understand my unfortunate journey better to this strange land.

Immediately, I reached the conclusion that the two men that brought me to this camp followed the "Ahia attack" trail but instead of dealing on food items and essential items they deal in human (women) trafficking. Moving women from one location to the other for soldiers and "selling" them for money, food items, salt, dried milk, dried egg and essential commodities. I also understand that they usually set up links in various communities. I wondered how they got to me and their link in my village that told them that they can get an orphan girl, in the early hours of the morning, under the Udara tree. Sometimes I will cry but most times I will remember my grandfather Pa Ugochukwu, who will always say "Evil Men Do Exist and they will always get their reward "and the biblical quotation from Sister Mary's Presbyterian Sunday school that, "patience is a virtue".

I started looking for a copy of the Bible to build my faith and stay strong. I knew this will help me keep strong and alive so that I will survive.

I finally had the courage to ask Captain James, who gave me a copy of his personal Bible. He asked me to read it only in the room. He warned that some of the junior military men that serve him are Muslims and can report me to the others.

The human rights abuses of many Igbo civilians through the alleged use of airstrikes, starvation policy, and sexual crimes against young girls and women continued and was being discussed quietly among the girls and young women.

The girls and women of the other minority groups such as the Ogoni, Efik, Ibibio, Annang, Ogoja, and Ekoi suffered even more atrocities. Many neighboring Biafra communities saw them as saboteurs hence they will always arrange the local soldiers to attack them and loot their properties. These soldiers sometimes will end up killing their men, raping their women and stealing from them. These group of Igbo neighbors suffered in the hands of the Nigerian troops as well as Biafran soldiers.

People in the camp were not blind nor deaf to what was going on. The acts which destroy the dignity of thousands of young girls and women were not hidden. They were considered the "spoils of war."

I kept mostly to myself and related with people who were kind to me. I related also with girls and women primarily to learn and know what was going on. I listen more and more and learnt many unbelievable incidences.

For months, Captain James was feeling sorry for me. Each time he goes to the war front he will tell his cook and other loyal men to look out for me, until he gets back, and he will tell me to take care of myself and not go out from his quarters.

During one of his war assignments, after about three months of my arrival, I discovered that I was looking forward to his coming back and every time he was not around, I will pray for his safe journey and safe return.
Upon his return, I noticed he was moody and sad.

I wondered why.

The cook told me that Captain James' Army unit lost many men in a crossfire with the Biafran soldiers. His unit advanced into a farmer's field in an early morning push. Unknown to them, a set of Biafran soldiers lay in wait.... Then followed a barrage of fire and explosive sounds of the ingenious Biafra cluster bombs called "Ogbunigwe". The attacks wiped out a lot of the Nigerian soldiers, including his friends and some course mates.

His unit was so angry that they spent the next two days "focused on bombing the hell out of the Biafra soldiers." They destroyed the Nkana Bridge with their "Ogbunigwe". There were causalities on both sides.

On that moonless night, I heard him cry.
Prayerfully, and in sadness, he asked: "God, why so much killings?"

Although Captain James bore no physical wounds when he returned, the burden was so heavy, he had a savage mix of guilt over the fallen and an unrelenting feeling of responsibility for the living.

Also, he struggled with nightmares, rage and grief long after they returned to the camp. Their team was given 3 days off the zones of direct combat. They were to recoup and get themselves emotionally ready for another assignment.

It was during this period that one night he came to me and asked me:

"Can I teach you certain things about your body?"
I didn't know what to say. I did not know what to do. I did not have a choice but to oblige him.

I said to myself that if he had not protected me all these months, I would have ended up being a "public property" — shared by different men of all ages.

The stories I heard from others in the camp about the deliberate humiliation, psychological warfare of sexual slavery, deliberate

and forceful intrusion of girls and women were scary....
I have been praying: "It will not be my portion."

I pondered and I rationalized that since no one knows who will die first, it's better giving out my virginity to this kind, gentle and caring man. After all, no one is sure what will happen next....

I had started falling in love with Captain James, praying for him and hoping that one day when things normalize and there is no more war that we can live together as family.

It was time to return to the battle fields of this war, for him. They went to war, and came back three weeks later. By his return, I was very sick. I kept managing, not wanting to reveal to anybody until Captain James came back.

On his return, I was eventually taken to the sick bay/make-shift clinic. The army Doctor performed series of test and confirmed I was pregnant.

Captain James was very happy and told me that his parents will be excited. I was scared, hence, I kept asking myself: "How I can be pregnant when I'm not even thirteen years old?"

Not sure what will become of me, I kept the information to myself. He made sure that he collected medications for me.

At this time I started keeping more to myself, trying to hide away from the glare of evil eyes, knowing the different things that I have heard of what they do to babies in the camp.

I was introduced to Papa Akpan's wife. She sells fish near the stream. She will be my pregnancy guide and direct me on what to do. I was asked to be open to her to tell her any problem I may have. Nkoyo was a good woman and an inspiration to me. She encouraged me to eat more and told me not to talk to many people.

She told me the stories of babies being taken away from captured women and girls and suggested that when it is time for my delivery that she will prefer a local maternity lady to deliver the baby instead of the going to the military clinic.
She cautioned that "this will minimize the chances of someone taking the baby to sell and telling you that your baby died...."

When Captain James came back Papa Akpan also told him the same. I was instructed not to tell anyone my due date. By the time people noticed I was pregnant, I was almost full term, but I kept saying I believe I am about three or four months pregnant. Captain James made arrangements with Papa Akpan for him to take me to a different village where a local maternity woman can deliver the baby when the time comes. Each time Captain James was around he will make it clear that he preferred the treatment from the local maternity. He made arrangements with the nurse so that I will still be collecting my medications.

I made sure that I eat well as instructed by Madam Nkoyo. I eat vegetables and mostly meat and I even noticed how well nourished, strong and happy. I was looking forward to bringing in a new life into the world.

I had my baby during one of the rainy nights in late June.
To me, it was long and difficult delivery but to the Mama maternity nurse, it is expected for first babies.

Aunty Nkoyo Akpan and Papa Akpan were the only people who had knowledge of the birth of the baby boy. They asked me for the name that will be given to the baby.

I did not have any.

I told them "I will wait for the Captain to come and name the baby."

I spent one week there, and Mr. Akpan had to go back and manage the expectations of those at the camp by telling them I was sick and spending time with the local maternity nurse who was giving me herbs.

I bonded with my baby during this period as I fell in love with my baby boy, who came during my trial period and storm to give me comfort. His birth gave me another reason to live and renewed my decision to survive against all odds.

Captain James obtained permission from the war front, came back and privately came to visit at me. He was delighted and thrilled that God has surprised him and his family with a son.

He named him James, too.

He muttered in his breath that "He is that son that will take over from me."

For his middle and ethnic name, he chose to call him Ali (meaning excellent and noble).

He asked me if I have an Igbo name for him, and I immediately said Onyekachi (Nobody is greater than God).

It was my way of thanking God for covering and protecting me against the evil of men and still have faith that no matter what happens to me or Captain James that God is supreme.
JAMES ALI ONYEKACHI BANFA

The birth of my son was an amazing experience for me. Looking into the eyes of my baby, a lot was communicated between us. The expressiveness of his eyes brought me strength, even in the midst of my situation. I felt complete, satisfied and blessed.

Captain James spent the next two weeks taking care of us. During this period, he opened up to me about who he is. Born in the village of Langtan in Plateau state by two Christian teachers. His town is in the southern part of Plateau State, near Jos.

His father was a Chemistry teacher who later became a Principal of a school, while his mom was a primary school teacher. They both wanted him to go to school and excel. When the war broke out, he enlisted in the army and was trained at the Nigerian Defense Academy, Kaduna, before he went out to fight the war.

He was influenced by the many prominent military officers from his hometown who made or were still making remarkable impact on the lives of people in his community.

He said he wanted to be like them and contribute positively to the lives of people.

The man paused. He paused to reflect on what he, evidently, has been thinking about telling me.....

He noted that although he was almost 20 years older than me that when the war ends, he would make things right. He promised and basically was asking me "to consider marrying him."

Before I could take in his awkward proposal, he continued: "if you accept me, I'll send you back to school to continue your studies."

He asked: "What would you like to study?"

I quickly said: "Nursing."

I narrated to him the various experiences of the children of Biafra, on the other side of the river. He was surprised but I told him that it was influenced with what I witnessed in my hometown.

In most Biafran towns and villages, we witnessed a disease called Kwashiokor, which is a form of severe malnutrition, due to lack of protein. Many children and adults who suffer from this ailment are bloated.

According to Uloma's dad who is a nurse in my village, the bloating is as a result of excess fluid trapped within tissues of the body, and this causes swelling of hands, arms, feet, ankles, leg and the belly.

He also told us that vital organs such as the liver are enlarged due to insufficient protein consumption. Other symptoms include changes of skin and hair color to a rust color and texture, fatigue, diarrhea, loss of muscle mass, failure to grow or gain weight; damaged immune system, which can lead to more frequent and severe infections and irritation.

When I become a nurse, I would like to work with Uloma's dad and help to treat Nkechi and other kids suffering from Kwashiokor. Many children from my town suffered from it. My uncle who came back from Umuahia sometimes said it is common among Biafran children all over.

I did not want to take my son back to then Republic of Biafra to avoid him, potentially, suffering from Kwashiokor. He was surprised to hear all these. While the lives of the Federal troops and other regions continue to be normal, the lives of innocent Biafrans were like living in hell, full of hunger and malnutrition.

He told me that "Although, our federal troops have the upper hand, in terms of equipment and resources, nobody knows what will happen as the final outcome of the war. But whatever happens, promise that if anything happens to me, please take our son home to my people; just in case I do not survive this war."

Captain James took the baby and I back to the camp after a while. He spent few days before leaving again to the war front, but before he left, he asked his loyal staff to make sure that they watch over us and to report any suspicious activity to the authorities.

Prior to going back to the war front, Captain James was worried for his son and for me, hence he had planned for the local maternity woman to visit us at the camp periodically to take care of me and the baby James. I later discovered that he told Papa Akpan to be watchful over us and he gave Akpan the full name of his family, his village and direction. He said, should he "be a casualty from the war, please take my son to my village and find a way to take Ije back to her home in Arochukwu."

4
THE TRIP
BACK HOME
AND THE
END OF
THE WAR

Papa Akpan was a retired police officer who was still strong to support the local Nigerian army who had invaded his village after the fall of Calabar and Annang Provinces. He was one of the elders who came out of the bush and intervened to prevent the Nigerian Troops from killing their people. He and other elders volunteered to assist the troops in any way they can, which later resulted to giving them free food supplies and medication. They do not go to war front, neither were they soldiers but local vigilantes supporting the troops to protect their homes and people. He had worked in the Northern Nigeria region for years, prior to the start of the war. His family relocated from Kano, Northern Nigerian, when the southerners were being massacred in the Northern Nigeria. His brother who was a businessman and his cousin did not make it out of Kano during the 1966 pogrom where the main targets were the Igbo and other south Eastern persons.

He suffered the pains of the war and he knew how difficult it will be for a young, thirteen (13) year old girl to be alone, during a war in a strange land with a little baby. He felt very sorry for me.

Many of the Northern soldiers around were not aware that he understood and spoke impeccable Hausa language. The knowledge of the language helped Akpan to understand what the lower level soldiers discuss in the canteen and in various locations.

One of those days Papa Akpan went to deliver drinks to the army canteen, he overheard some soldiers speaking in Hausa and talking about the causalities they had in the war front the previous night. Captain James' name was mentioned but Papa Akpan pretended as if he did not hear what they were whispering.

Papa Akpan went home immediately and told his wife, they now came up with a plan to assist me and the baby. An arrangement was made for his sister in-law, Idong, to go and get me and baby

James at dusk and take us to another village for safety. Unfortunately, by the time their sister Idong got there, two strange hooded men had walked in demanding for the baby and disappeared with my baby! Despite my yelling, crying and shouting, they snatched my baby James from my hand and disappeared in the dusk of the night.....

Shocked, traumatized and consumed with feeling of hopelessness I threw myself on the floor, shouting and crying, trying to comprehend and process what just happened.

I was still crying, sobbing, wondering what to do when sister Idong came in through the back door. Shocked and surprised I narrated to her what has transpired. Idong encouraged me to get ready quickly and gather a few necessary things for the journey. My initial reaction was to say "no way, and I will not leave without my baby."

Then, Idong told me of the rumors of the death of Captain James. The next thing they will do to me at the camp will be to circulate you among the different military men, and that my best option is to go with her to her great grandmother's home, which is located in a village 8 miles away. She also confirmed to me that from there I will join the traders who go to the nearest Biafra controlled areas to sell salt and other items.

With that disguise I can go back home to my town, Arochukwu. We both know it will be a difficult and daunting journey but a better option than staying in the camp without my baby and without Captain James.

I felt lost, hollow, depressed and lifeless. I cried and cried but decided to control myself and go for my only sensible option of trusting sister Idong, whom I had met many times at the Akpans.

I rushed into the room, opened the cabinet with the key, collected all the money from the cabinet, packed some salt, dried milk and eggs and through the back down we disappeared into the night and ran and ran.

We ran and walked for hours before she said this is my grandmother's village. When we got to her grandmother's compound, sister Idong headed to the window of one of the old thatched houses and knocked hard on the window. An elderly woman opened the window first asked who it was, Idong called out her name and she opened the door without asking any more questions.

The elderly grandmother did not ask many questions, rather she gave us water to drink. Idong said to me, this village is called "Ikoro Abasi "and this old mama is my grandmother. Members of my village go to Market in many Arochukwu plantains such as Mbiaobong, Nturi, and Asioekpo across the river. The traders that go to sell salt, hot drink, cigarettes, dried eggs and milk, dried meat, dried fish sometimes go on daily basis but mostly go on the market days of the plantations.

For the traders to cross, they pay the Nigerian troops on this side and after they cross, they pay the Biafra soldiers who are very hungry and always look forward to seeing them because the traders pay them by giving them cigarettes and food suppliers especially salt.

She asked me, "Are you familiar with the plantations?" I said: "No."

She added: "Once you cross the river with them to that side you can ask questions and find your way home. You can stay here for few days until the market day. Nobody can find you here — if you do not go out."

On that market day, I was made up, dressed like an old lady and warned not to say anything. Their grandmother handed me over to another auntie called Eka, who's familiar with the terrain.

We proceeded with the women traders, crossed the Nigerian soldiers at the boarder after bribing them with money and then we boarded a wooden boat operated by the local villagers and crossed the river. The Biafra soldiers who already saw us coming were waiting eagerly as they were waiting to receive gift items such as salt, local hot drinks and cigarettes. We crossed the corridor after giving them gift items. They were tattered, hungry Biafra soldiers who were willing and happy to collect anything from us, without any issues.

When we got to the other side of the river, I noticed that the local fish market was full of women and young adults, selling and buying different items. The language is Annang but mixed with Igbo.

I heard some women haggling prices in igbo language and the lady that accompanied me said this is Mbiaobong market. This area is a plantation of the Arochukwu people. She added "I will talk to Mazi Nkebem's wife. She goes to Arochukwu market every nkwo at the Obinkita Market Square. She is a good woman and will help you." I was surprised to hear the woman speak like that and called nkwo Obinkita market Square with ease. She told me, not to be surprised, that she is an Obinkita woman married to a man in Ikoro Abasi. Her Igbo name is Mgbeke but I prefer to answer Ekaete, in my husband's home place.

Idong told me "You are my sister, hence I decided to help you. I will tell her that you got home safely."

She advised me to send a message through her to Idong, anytime I want to reach them through Mazi Nkebem's wife. She also held me tight and encouraged me to take care of myself, not despair, and "hopefully your son will be found one day."

She also advised me "You've to be strong and do not share your story with any one. You should not trust people, especially during this war."

She added: "In times of war, people will do anything to eat, even sell their own folks, just to survive!"
She told me "to continue to pray for your son, God will place him right back in your hands."

I was kept hidden in one of their rooms for two days. Mazi Nkebem's wife Nma told me that there are many saboteurs and informants and such we need to be careful.

Overtaken by grief and sorrow, I felt a gut sinking feeling that spreads from my heart to other extremities. Overwhelmed by the feeling of loss of both Captain James and my son, I could not eat not, sleep well, nor think straight but happy that I got out of that environment.

Nma, noticed my mood and crying so she counseled me about keeping strong, ignore my pain and move on.
Two days later, Mazi Nkebem's wife, Nma, went with me to the Obinkita market. I was so excited to be home. The Air in Arochukwu, as usual, is always fresh, different.

On getting to Obinkita, I could not wait to go straight to the small road from the market square to Amankwu, Amoba, Ugbo, Amukwa and to my lovely village, Atani (nmawuru), the home of the strong heroes of Arochukwu.

On getting closer to the Atani hall, I could not help but sob for my son, for myself, for the lost months, for the physical and psychological trauma I had been through.
But beyond all those, I remained grateful to God for my returning home, alive!

Upon stepping into uncle Ogwo's compound, one of the girls heading for an errand saw me and started screaming, in joyful surprise. Folks in the compound who heard her shout rushed out to find out what was happening. They welcomed me. They were eager to hear my story....

———————/////—————————

My aunty was quick to ask, before I took a shower, "My daughter, what would you like to eat? I have your favorite vegetable soup with ukazi, watercress, periwinkle and fresh fish...."
Before she could mention the alternative of rice and stew, I affirmed "My favorite, ma. Thank you, ma."

About 8 minutes into my meal, more than 10 persons started gathering inside the parlour, and around it. They were anxiously waiting to hear my story! What happened, when and why? What did I experience on "the other side"?

With her experience as a mother, my aunt held a curious look at what she could tell where physiological changes for a young girl who had experienced sexual activity beyond her age. She, sensitively, did not want to jump to any hasty conclusions.

Afterwards, I told my story without mentioning that I had given birth to a son. I did not mention my relationship with Captain James Banfa. I kept my pain inside....

As I struggled with settling back into Atani, my mind was flooded with a lot of challenges and thoughts about where I had returned from; especially my son. Regardless, I continued to reintegrate amidst bouts of psychological problems.

I maintained contact with Mazi Nkebem's wife, who lives at Mbiaobong. After a couple of weeks, I started going to the Mbiaobong market to buy fish, which my auntie and I will resale at the Nkwo market or daily Obinkita market.

During these trips I am able to exchange messages with aunty Idong, Papa Akpan and Mrs. Akpan.

It is almost two and half months and there was no trace of my son. I still held on to my faith had hope that someday, soon, God will bring two of us together.

It has been 100 days, without any favorable feedback on my son!

My aunt remained curious and felt that there was more to my story....

After a lot of contemplation, I found strength and courage to trust my auntie Nwaka with my full story.

She felt very sad but encouraged me to keep my hope up and to move on with my life.

The Civil war started in 1967 with Col Emeka Odumegwu-Ojukwu, the military governor of the then Eastern Region inhabited mainly by Igbo people, accusing the federal government of marginalizing and killing thousands of ethnic Igbos and eastern regioners resident in the North. This resulted in then Col. Chukwuemeka Odumegwu-Ojukwu declaring the former Eastern Region a sovereign and independent Republic of Biafra on May 30, 1967.

This decision to create a "safe zone" was vehemently rejected by the federal authorities. After diplomatic efforts by Nigeria failed to reunite the country, war broke out in July 1967 between Nigeria and the much smaller and poorly equipped Biafran soldiers (mainly volunteers). The Biafra's forces made some initial advances, but Nigeria's superior military strength gradually reduced the Biafran territory. Nigerian military attacked all the border towns of the eastern region.

By the time the Nigerian forces captured the provincial capital of Owerri, one of the last Biafran strongholds, as well as Umuahia, the last capital of Biafra, Ojukwu was forced to flee to the west African country of Ivory Coast.
Many of our folks were ambivalent and cautious.
In the struggle for safety, it took my family days several days to

come out of the bushes, in January 1970 — after the war came to an abrupt end....

The bombing, shelling and penetration of Biafran towns and villages persisted in every direction. Soldiers, recruits and civilians defending various parts of Biafra 1 and 2 were coming home, as there was no safer town or camp.

The threat to overrun my hometown was imminent. The loud shelling and firing were coming closer and closer, every day.
On that fateful morning in Arochukwu, the enemy shelling was coming from different directions. Speculations were that the Federal troops have entered Arochukwu and were killing people in ime Aro (the inner, upper valley sections of the kingdom).

Biafran soldiers from Arochukwu who escaped from their duty post ran home to warn their families to run into the bushes or anywhere for safety. The federal troops were expected to come in from Nmaku, but they came in from Ito. A surprising, tactical maneuver. Especially, as the federal troops escalated the shelling.

There was pandemonium and chaos everywhere. Different families ran to different places. We ran to the bush, toward the farmland trails of Atani or Uzo ubi Atani.

Many families in Arochukwu ran to different places, as there was no co-ordinated movement. After some days, we got the news of impending Nigerian army victory. But that was received with mixed feelings.

Most people could not believe the news trickling in of how the federal troops entered Aro through Ito....

The Commander-in-Chief of the armed forces of the Republic of Biafra, Major-General Chukwuemeka Odumegwu Ojukwu and some of his key advisers had fled to Ivory Coast, in his own words,

"In search of peace". Our beloved Biafran leader, Ojukwu, left the country on January 8, 1970 a period Ojukwu assigned his deputy, Major General Phillip Effiong, from Ibiono Ibom, in the current Akwa Ibom State of Nigeria, to handle the affairs of Biafra.

Effiong, who assumed leadership in this situation of turmoil, starvation, and collapse, was announced as acting Head of State of Biafra. Then, on January 12, 1970, he announced through a speech broadcast on radio the surrender of Biafra!

Even the plants, birds, and the animals in the thick tropical rain forest of Arochukwu and the entire Biafra nation were silent. Silence engulfed the environment; the fledgling nation. Surrender!?
The Republic of Biafra ceased to exist and Gen. Yakubu Gowon, the leader of the federal government, famously declared that there was "no victor, no vanquished."

The first group of people that came home were those that ran to the bushes, like us. Many of the women and young girls were sent back into the bush, as there were news that the soldiers were taking girls and women and forcing them to go to their camps for forced sexual gratification....

Those that ran to other nearby towns of Ihechiowa, Ututu and Ohafia started coming home, in small sets, gradually.

Some of their family members were missing.

During the confusion of the sudden announcement of the "cessation of hostilities", some believed beyond Umuahia that Biafra was still in existence and that they could cross the corridor of the Nigerian soldiers who had blocked the roads and some villages to meet their Biafran kith and kin, on the other side of Biafra.

It was fatal; many families lost lives. On our way coming home from the bush, we saw dead bodies riddled with gun shots, the impact of bombs and the human evidence of hunger.

The horrific experiences of Biafra (1967-1970) during this period were devastating and sickening to the human mind and senses. The smell of dead bodies remained in the air for weeks. The horrific sight of vultures devouring dead (human) bodies was something I will never forget until the day I die.

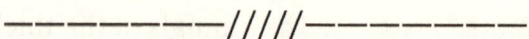

The memories of war can be very harsh; especially this war. Stories of the pains of the war abound from different villages.

On getting back to our home, I could hear different families crying, yelling for their loved one who possibly had been killed, missing or could not be accounted for.

My good friend Uloma's brother, who was first in the Nigerian army and a commissioned Lieutenant, waiting to go to Sandhurst Military College, England, and who later became a Major in the Biafra army due to the war, was killed in our village because he refused to acknowledge the presence of the Nigerian soldiers, who had asked him to surrender and lie face down....

After shooting him on the neck they stormed into their house and looted all their important belongings. He was among "the best of the best" in the Biafra army. An officer and a perfect gentleman. The family was grieving. Their mom cried, uncontrollably. Their father was a London trained nurse who not only treated people free but also gave them free relief food and things such as salt.

Our aunty Nnenna lost two of her very handsome and intelligent sons.

The war had a devastating impact on the citizens of Biafra. It resulted in the loss of millions of lives, of properties, means of livelihood.

Women and young girls were raped and most importantly many suffered the loss of their loved ones. It was a war of genocide against the Igbo/Easterners/Biafrans since 1966. Young, teenage and barely trained "soldiers" were conscripted to fight on the different war fronts. Civilians were subjected to bombing of their markets, schools, churches, hospitals, refugee camps.... They faced land, sea, aerial blockades. Finally, the inhuman imposition of starvation by Nigeria's government against Biafrans became too much to bear, too much to handle....

The land of the rising sun that we loved and cherished was no more. Our heroes could no longer defend the lives of its citizens. People who swore to die without a shred of fear were tired of the smell of death, hence felt that spilling of more blood will no longer be a sensible thing to do. The war recorded the death of more than two million civilians, mostly due to starvation.

We came out of the ordeal not triumphantly, but with the wounds of the war. We started our lives from the scratch, waiting to heal.... I came out of that war with the pain of losing Captain James and my son baby James.

5
BACK TO SCHOOL AND END OF THE WAR

B efore the war, our in-law, Mazi Ogwo, was a contractor with one of the local administrative units in Aba. Hence, shortly after the war ended, he decided to go back to Aba — alone, first. Then, return to get his family.

Things were very difficult for everyone. Aunty Nwaka stayed in the village with all of us to continue her trade. Money was scare as Biafra currency was not accepted as legal tender for trade. Biafrans who had hundreds and thousands and millions of Pounds/money in banks were given only twenty pounds each. This was regardless of the size of their Bank accounts, however a few of those who had bank accounts in some parts of Nigeria were allowed to operate those account without loss of value. All civil servants, traders and most contractors fell into the previous category. Uncle Ogwo was not an exception. The money he got was grossly inadequate to take care of the family.

I encouraged Aunty Nwaka to commence selling fish from Mbiaobong, Nturi and Asioekpo. I also joined in the fish trading business. Using part of the Nigerian currency which I got from the private cabinet drawer inside Captain James' room the day I left the Nigerian military camp, I encouraged my aunt to travel with me across the river in Ikot Offiong. It was from here that we started buying and selling fish. The fish business favored us. I used my connection with Mazi Nkebem's wife from Mbiaobong, effectively.

Throughout the remainder of 1970, my cousin Ngo and I did not go to school, rather I followed aunty Nwaka to the various plantation markets and bought items for resell in Aro and the nkwo market in Obinkita. People knew us as credible and honest fish sellers and we saved money in preparation for Ngozi and I to go back to school the next year. During the market periods in Mbiaobong, I used it as an opportunity to exchange information with my contacts and to keep my ears open for my son, hoping that one day there will be good news.

In 1971, we all joined uncle Ogwo in Aba. I started secondary school at Community Girls Secondary School, Umungasi, Aba. The school was formerly, Immaculate Girls secondary school. It was founded in the year 1961 by the Catholic Mission, under the leadership of Bishop Nwedo. With the government takeover of schools in 1970, the names of the school changed to Community Secondary school.

Aba is a city in the southeast of Nigeria and the commercial center of Eastern Nigeria (Aba is the largest town in Abia State). The town lies along the west bank of the Aba River (Waterside) and is at the intersection of roads leading to Port Harcourt, Owerri, Umuahia, Ikot Ekpene and Ikot Abasi.

Aunty Nwaka's house was not far from the school, hence Ngozi and I usually wake up very early to help her prepare "kpuff kpuff", "chin chin", rice, beans, plantain, "akara" and "moi moi" which she sells, mostly, to artisans and students.

Her eatery became very popular with students; and because he was a very good cook her food items would finish early. With that modest income, she was able to support her husband and train us in school. Seeing how hardworking and useful Ngozi and I were, uncle Ogwo took and accept us as family.

In 1976, I prepared for my West African School Certificate exams and passed with flying colors.

I always wanted to read and practice nursing, hence I applied and sat for the national exam for student nurses and passed. I was lucky to be placed in my first choice, University of Nigeria Teaching hospital, Enugu, (UNTH). The program commenced in 1977 for my Nursing program for three years.

My grades and appraisals were good enough that I was one of those selected ones from my class for the Bachelor of Science in Nursing, (BSN) program.

As a teaching hospital that is affiliated to the University of Nigeria, Nsukka, it was easy for the good students of the teaching hospital to move to the degree program after the three-years Registered Nurse (RN) program.

On my Bachelor of Nursing graduation, aunty Nwaka, uncle Ogwo and Ngozi came all the way from Aba to the University of Nigeria, Nsukka. They were proud of me and I was proud of myself. I wished my grandfather Pa Ugochukwu were still alive, he would have been so proud of me. As I marched with other students in the large Margaret Ekpo hall of the University, I was excited, happy and grateful to God for bringing me this far.

Amid happiness and jubilation, I remembered my past and pain that will always haunt my heart, my baby James and wondered what he will look like now, if alive. He would have been sixteen years, in this year of 1985. I prayed silently for him and committed him into the hands of the God Almighty!

After the graduation march, a young Medical Doctor, Nnaemeka Ogbuagu who three months ago concluded his residency in orthopedic surgery had actively expressed his "serious interest to know more about" me also attended the graduation on my invitation. He walked up to me to congratulate me and meet my family. I introduced them and warmly referred to Nnaemeka as "a friend." Ngozi chuckled....

He took us to the Continuing Education Center (CEC) for a very good lunch. We chatted, generally. My folks liked him. Later that evening, my aunt called me and "wanted to know more about that young man."

She encouraged me, stating, without mincing words, "if you love him, you should not wait too long — since a woman's time for childbirth is limited." She advised that I "should make hay while the sun shines."

I heard her loud and clear, but I had a secret burden that I had carried on for years, and I prayed that I will sort it out first before proceeding on marriage.

After the graduation event, we returned to Aba. After a couple of days, I travelled to my village. After my village visit, on my way back I decided to take the Ikot Ekpene axis, primarily to stop over at Ikoro Effiong to visit Papa Akpan's family. They were delighted to see me.

Unfortunately, Papa Akpan had passed on after suffering from hepatitis. His wife took me to his grave, which was in front of their house. After praying, she told me how sorry she was that they could not assist me further in locating my son. She, however, mentioned that her husband continued investigating; and discovered that one of those two men who came to the camp that night to steal the baby was a local hoodlum named Ufot Essien who had bragged about it after he was drunk.

Papa Akpan approach him one day he was sober to ask him what happened to baby James. Essien revealed that one of the military corporals who visited the camp from Assang sector had confided in him that he was looking for the baby boy and that a Nigerian Army Colonel in the Assang sector committed to pay a large sum of money if he can find the baby.

Essien confirmed that he eventually led the Corporal from Assang sector to "find the right baby."

He also confirmed that the Corporal was aware of the demise of Captain James, the father of the baby.

"When Essien told my husband this story, he was sober, sad and upset as the corporal never compensated him for his role in stealing the baby. Essien unfortunately, did not know the name of the Colonel from Assang sector nor why he wanted this particular baby. Essien was used by this strange man he met at the local bar. By the time Essien made this confession to my husband, the war had long ended, everyone had gone, there was no way of tracing the Colonel, but he did mention that the Colonel was from the North. My husband took a trip to Assang sector of the war, no individual could remember this Colonel's name."

This update was devastating to me and my mission of reconnecting with baby James was dashed....

During my trip back, I spent time on the road from Ikoro Abasi to Aba, Owerri and Enugu, planning on what next steps to take. Tired of carrying the albatross around my neck, I took a decision to open up to my fiancé Dr. Nnaemeka as the burden was too much for me to carry. I felt that if he loves me, he should help me carry this burden or help me in finding solution to the problem. I, finally, confided in him and he immediately understood my predicament.

He promised to help me.

I accepted to marry him and build a family with him, primarily because I love him. Secondly, because he accepted to assist me to search for my son....

6
THE LOKOJA FAMILY OF DANLADI HAMZA

In the middle belt of Nigeria, the town where the two largest rivers in West Africa, River Niger and River Benue meet is called Lokoja. The two rivers form a Y-shaped confluence in what appears to be a magnificent union and draining southwards into the Atlantic Ocean.

In this town, the rivers are major sources of economic activities for inhabitants and business-minded persons in search of opportunities. Some of them reside across the rivers' banks.
As hospitable ecological locations, they offer natural habitats for aquatic animals and other species.

At that confluence in Lokoja were beautiful landscapes set across the calm water, alongside a green vegetation.

Lokoja was a hub for the migration of thousands who had to flee the attacks on the indigenous peoples around the middle belt set upon by the radical Jihadist who followed Usman Dan Fodio into parts of the region in the early 19th century.

Also, Lokoja and its neighboring communities has several families of successfully retired officers of the Nigerian armed forces who established cotton farms, fisheries, tomatoes and other farming products, such as leather, palm oil and palm kernel.

One of those families had their farming products shipped to the Niger delta ports of Warri and Burutu for export. Their sixteen-year-old first son, Dahiru was planning for his graduation from Command Children School, Chari Maigumeri Barracks, Lokoja and how to go to the Military College. Dahiru preferred the Air Force Military School in Jos, in Plateau State but his mother discouraged him from going to any military college rather persuaded him to go to a medical school, since he was good in science subjects. His mother, Sirkina Zang, was very proud of his academic achievements. He was an all-rounder, good in both science and arts. His mother's argument remained that military career was risky and that many of the top middle belt military men have been killed in coups and counter coups....

Dahiru was her only child that she would not want him to be exposed to that.

Unknown to Dahiru she had many reasons for not wanting him to serve in the military, hence she encouraged him to apply to medical school abroad, preferably United Kingdom. He applied and successfully obtained admission for medical studies in the UK.

While at school, he met many Nigerians from different parts of the country and befriended many Igbos, Yoruba and his fellow Hausas from the mid-North, some Fulani Muslims, and some Christians.

The Nigerian Student Union activities exposed him to many people, and he began to learn more about different cultures, different religions and came to a conclusion that people from different parts of Nigerian have things that are more in common that things that are different. He reflected back to the war stories his parents told him, how many of the stories were focused on how they are different from the other ethnic groups across the river, behind the mountains, and across the valley. He resolved that when he completes his schooling in England, that he would want to work in a more urban and heterogeneous location like Lagos or Abuja.

During his final year in Medical School, his mother was admitted into the hospital due to a stage four uterine cancer. She knew she might not live long enough but if anything happened to her she had packed and kept two boxes of her precious personal items and some important messages with her sister Fatima. Fati, as she was fondly called, was a beautiful lady that served his mom when Dahiru was a kid. One of his father's uncles married sister Fati. Ever since, she has been like a second mother to Dahiru. He was heartbroken and prayed to God to keep his mom alive until he became a Medical Doctor. He wanted this beautiful, kind, considerate Mom to witness his graduation.

The Lord granted him his wish. His parents came for his graduation and during that period his mom repeated what she said before and asked him to forgive her — if he discovers that she has "in any way done anything against" him.

He least expected that from his lovely mom but promised her that there is nothing he will hear that will ever make him not to love her. That was the last time he saw his mom alive. She died peacefully at home after that trip and was buried within 24 hours of her death according to Muslim tradition.

Dahiru flew to Lokoja for her burial. After the burial, Fati invited him to have Lunch with her and her family the next day, Dahiru accepted knowing how close she was with his mom. After the lunch, Fati took Dahiru to a private room, showed him two big boxes and gave him a set of keys. Dahiru was so emotional to even open the boxes, hence he told her to keep them safely for him, until next time when he is in the right frame of mind to open them. She accepted and went into an adjoining inner room, where she brought out a crafted unique handbag and handed it to Dahiru, "This is also from your mom. She said the information in this bag is far more important than anything in the boxes. I do not know what is there but whatever is in this bag, please read it, they are her wishes."

Dahiru took the bag from her, thanked her and went home. On getting home, Dahiru opened the bag and saw letters and unique items but decided to read them when he is alone.

Dahiru's father's mansion is a magnificent house on three floors with a total of 14 rooms. With three other wives and nine other children, the house was always full of people. Each of the three other wives live in their own quarters or section, just like flats or apartments. Each section had three bedrooms, plus a living room.

Each section has two toilets and bathroom. While the mothers stayed in their self-contained rooms with bath and toilets, the children stay in the other rooms, sharing baths and toilets. Mini kitchen with appliances and a store are also attached to each apartment. The main living room downstairs is specifically for visitors with an adjoining kitchen, library and a dining hall that can seat 30 people. The apartments for the other three wives were all on the first floor, while the second floor was the penthouse, which has a living room, Dahiru's father's Master's room, his mom's Madam's room and Dahiru's own section with two specials rooms, all self-contained.

On the right side of the house are five guest rooms for family and friends, plus laundry and the family kitchen. On the back toward the orchard tress are four self-contained quarters for service staff.
At night when everyone has gone to bed, the penthouse was quiet, his dad had received many visitors during that next day after his mom's burial and decided to retire to his section early.

Dahiru reached for the bag to see the items inside it. He opened one of the letters addressed to him, in his mother's handwriting.

His mother first apologized to Dahiru "for not having the courage to tell you certain things" when she was alive. She praised him. "Dahiru, you're my world. Thank you for having given my life so much happiness and joy, from the very first day you were brought to me!"
"Brought to her?" Dahiru repeated in utter shock, in his mind; he wondered what his mother was talking about.

He was perplexed.
Angry.
Confused.
Fear of the unknown story overcame him.

He rushed into the washroom to ease himself. He noticed that he needed to do more than pee; so he sat on the toilet seat. He continued to read the entire "confession and revelation" that narrated the story of how the Corporal brought him from the Ikoro Effiong area to the Assang war sector, how they immediately took Dahiru in as their son, since they could not have any child after five years of trying. She revealed how much they paid the Corporal. She "apologized for our actions" and warned Dahiru "please do not fight your Dad for what I planned and executed with him; rather be grateful that we kept and completely loved you as our own."

She appealed to Dahiru, in her closing paragraph, "I beg you not to disclose this information to any one as it will bring shame to your father and myself. It could or will make you lose all the inheritance you will gain as the first son of the Danladi Hamza family."

Dahiru paced, in agony, from the toilet to his room.

He continued to reflect on the implications of what he had just read. He now knew why he does not look like any of his parents, why his mom would not want him to play with other children when he was a kid, nor have close relationship with other family members. He wondered who else besides his father knew that he was not a biological son and not even adopted son, but rather a kidnapped boy, bought from a Corporal during the Nigeria-Biafra 1967-1970 War!

The strange news devastated him. He suspected that the other person who will know more was Fati, so he made up his mind to approach his father first; and Fati, the next day.

For the first time in his life, he felt unsafe and unsecured, so Dahiru locked his door from the inside. He recalled that he brought some sleeping pills from England. He took enough to assist him to sleep. The next morning, Dahiru heard this very consistent hard knock on the door, it was his father. He was leaving early to Abuja as he had a meeting with one of the big politicians and will be back the next day. Since he was already dressed and ready to go, he could not stop him. He enquired to know if Dahiru slept well and he responded by nodding his head but Dahiru observed the sadness on his face, which he attributed to the loss of his mother, his first wife. Dahiru's mother has always been his favorite wife. They both grew up in the same neighborhood and were not only lovers, but there is this brother and sister relationship they have shared together. To lose a wife of thirty-two (32 years) is not an easy emotional trauma.

Later that afternoon, Dahiru met with Fati, and pointedly asked her to tell him about his birth. Although, she wondered why, but she told him that he was born during the civil war in one of the war fronts and that was after five years of his parents' marriage. Fati continued:

"They lived happily for an additional seven years without issues, but when you were about twelve years, your father was advised by his family to get another wife and he did it for the reason to have more children. His second wife joined the family, and gave birth to three (3) sons and one (one) girl. The second wife felt that your father's attention to your mother was very obvious to everyone. The second wife believed that because she had many children, that she should be given prominence in the family more than your mother. That did not go well with Dahiru's mother, she then encouraged her husband to take a third and fourth wife." She told him that was "acceptable within the Muslim tradition, so that no one will feel more important than the other."

According to Fati, "This is why, there is major disparity in terms of your age and that of your other siblings."

Fati asked Dahiru "not to worry and that regardless of the fact that you're an only child of your mother, Allah has blessed you with intelligence, good looks and one day, you will get married and have many children, who will be members of your own nuclear family."

Dahiru immediately knew that Fati did not have a clue of his background, hence will not understand his pain, confusion and the "heavy burden of knowing where I came from and who my biological parents are."
Dahiru however thanked Fati for her love and consistent care. Dahiru left her concluding that she was not aware of what transpired and the circumstances surrounding how he ended up as a Lokoja Prince. Dahiru felt less proud of the man he has called his father for purchasing and snatching another person's child....

He was determined to confront him at the earliest opportunity.

7
DAHIRU CONFRONTS HIS FATHER

The next day, the retired Col. Danladi Hamza called to check up on his son, Dahiru. He informed him that he will be delayed for two or three days in Abuja before coming back.

Dahiru informed his father that he was coming to Abuja that day to meet with an old friend of his and that he can meet up with him the next day in his hotel. His father provided his hotel details to him. When Dahiru got to Abuja that day, he checked in that same hotel where his father was.

The next morning, Dahiru scheduled an early breakfast with his father and he immediately noticed that something was not right with his disposition and asked him what the problem was with him. He even noticed it that morning he woke him up and told him that he was going to Abuja.

Dahiru and his father have had a wonderful father-son relationship. He influenced his development into adulthood and his thinking process.   As a father, he has been Dahiru's most important role model, and has loved and supported Dahiru, unconditionally. It was a daunting task for Dahiru and a burden to challenge his father openly. Opening the Pandora box with his father now, especially when they are both mourning a loved one, but the quest to know who he is and how he ended up as Danladi Hamza's son, far outweighed the consequences of his feelings.

Dahiru proceeded. "Who am I, Dad?"
Without hesitation, he queried: "How did you find me and who are my birth parents?"

Dahiru asked with boldness, unblinking and unapologetic anger: "Who?"
Watching his father's non-verbal reaction from the corner of his eyes, Dahiru was stunned, his brows were knitted together, agonized and glazed. He was unable to speak and react normally.

As a Medical Doctor, Dahiru was aware of the consequences of confronting people with what they thought was a hidden sin. Dahiru demanded answers from his father. His reactions confirmed Dahiru's quest but Dahiru needed to hear more. It was difficult for Dahiru to speak to his father in a public place, so he requested for them to go to his room upstairs in a private place. They both got up from their seats concurrently, moved towards the elevator first and as Dahiru walked, his father followed sluggishly in a very slow motion, as if he was wondering on how to deal with this shock, knowing the truth. When they got into the elevator, his face was bleak, anxious and deadpan. Dahiru had never ever seen him look dejected and doleful like that. Dahiru decided to control his emotions in handling this delicate issue as he did not want to lose the parents he had known all his life within 12 days. Caution was the watchword for him, hence he decided to be cool, calm and to focus on the truth and the information he needed. It was not the time to play the blame game.

On getting to his suite, Dahiru called and ordered a bottle of Hennessy. As Muslims, they do not drink alcohol [at least, in public]. He has seen his father drink privately and he, too, drinks privately. His father's initial reaction was that there was no need for a drink, but he insisted that they both needed it to calm their nerves.

Prior to the arrival and serving of the drink, his father started the story: "Sometimes in life, one is faced with difficult challenges and it is not all the time that people know the right decision to take. First of all, your biological father was a very good friend of mine, an officer and gentleman whom I had trained in the army."

He continued: "We went to many successful battles together. Your biological father was a hardworking and intelligent young officer, James Banfa. He had potential for leadership position, hence he was sent on many training programs and eventually transferred to the Ikot Effiong sector. I met with him many times in Calabar

57

during the officers' training programs. During one of his trips from the Ikot Effiong sector to Assang sector, Captain James Banfa confided in me, about the young Igbo girl who had a handsome son for him, and that with what was going on during the war, nobody was sure of survival, and that if anything happens to him that he would want me, as his friend, to take his son home to his parents."

He recalled that "Banfa provided his family and village details; including the fact that he was a Christian from Langtan Village in the Jos area of Plateau State."

Then a knock on the door. They were interrupted by the hotel service staff who brought the drink and dropped it on the center table with two glasses, as requested.

He politely asked if he should open and serve the drink; his dad nodded in affirmation.

As soon as the door closed, he drank everything in his cup and looked at Dahiru with an edgy curiosity.

"Please continue", Dahiru exclaimed in a hoarse voice, wanting to hear and note every detail. He did; and added: "Immediately I received confirmation that the Captain died in the battle, I sent one of my trusted Corporals to go and look for the baby at the Ikot Effiong military camp and to, quietly, bring the baby to Assang sector, without anybody knowing. When the baby was brought to Assang sector, after some days, my late wife, who for the previous five years had been looking for a child found an opportunity to take care of a handsome healthy son. Our plan was to take you back to Captain James Banfa's family when the war ended, but your mother had started loving and training you as her own and had been telling people from the sector that you were her son.

"What of my birth mother?" Dahiru asked. Col. Hamza replied "I never knew her."

"How can this happen, and you and your wife got away with this?", Dahiru demanded?

"My son, there are many things you need to understand. During that war in Nigeria, just like most wars, a lot of unthinkable things do happen...."

As he continued talking, Dahiru was in utter shock. "Frankly, I do not know your biological mother, but she must have been one of the victims of the war. At that time, the women were not treated well nor recognized as wives even when they have the children."

With a reflective sense of agony, he said that "For your biological father to have pleaded with me to look for you, if anything happened to him, means that whoever your biological mother was, is someone he cherished and respected enough to want to keep her child. Even the women and girls who go through these traumas end up with the feeling of shame, humiliation, self-blame, and fear and sometimes reject the children born in this circumstance. This is one of the well-kept secrets of war that only exists in rumors and usually denied by the perpetrators and the victims."

He revealed that he was later informed that she was an Igbo young girl from the neighboring community of the Biafra area. Whether she survived the war or not, he did not know.

"How come, you did not take me to my father's people? Did he not have relatives?" Dahiru asked.

"Like I said earlier, my wife, your mother could not have a child, and she had gotten used to telling people at the Assang camp that you were her own, and she sent a message home telling people at home that God had finally blessed her with a son. We gave you the name Dahiru and registered your birth at the nearby local maternity hospital clinic and committed to take care of you for the rest of your life."

"You mean, you did not even legally adopt me. You just stole me from my original owners without signing any document and without paying?" Dahiru queried his father.

"What kind of friend of my biologically father are you, a friend that turned to become a thief after his friend died. What of my father's family, you had their information, why did you not send me to them", Dahiru added?

Hamza narrated how he visited Langtan during the chieftaincy title of one of the army Generals, and used the opportunity to find Captain James Banfa's family.

At the time he visited Langtan, town, Dahiru's biological grand-parents were old and poor, the family were delighted to see an old friend of their son. "After that meeting, I made sure that they received compensation from the army for the loss of their son., and from time to time I will send some money to them, but they are both late now. "

"There must be someone in that family that is still alive", Dahiru questioned. Hamza accepted that he had not kept in touch with them.

Confused, distraught, baffled at this weird tale, neither sure what to believe nor what to do, Dahiru stormed out of the room without saying a word.

He spent additional days in Abuja before going back to Lokoja to say goodbye to his friends and the other family members, especially Fati, as well as attend the seven day prayers for his late mother.

For the remainder of their days in Abuja, he refused to pick his father's calls. He figured that his father will be back in the village for the prayers.

His town and home where he has always loved was different now. Somehow, he felt he was a stranger, an unknown person, the product of the 1967-1970 war by an unknown mother and a dead soldier! Under those circumstances, he felt he did not fit in well in the mighty Danladi Hamza household. But he was able to conceal his pain.

Before leaving Lokoja, he decided to visit the confluence location of the two Rivers (Benue and Niger), a place he has visited many times. This time, he decided to go to the elevated position of the famed mount Patti. As he looked down, he saw boats and the ferries carrying people and an amazing sight of the colors of the two Rivers.

The River Niger water appears to be muddy and brownish in color while the River Benue water appears to be bluish green, showing clearly the difference in the two waters. This beautiful town where tourist and lovers of nature visit is a beauty to behold. The sight reminded him of something he heard many years ago about rivers. "The river will always flow, even in the midst of mountains."

8
THE MARRIAGE AND MY LIFE AFTER

My ancestral home Arochukwu, popularly called Aro, has a rich marriage tradition, which is as old as the kingdom itself. Marriage in my culture is between a man and a woman (and the families involved). It is a culture of nobility and decent celebration. Hence, the traditional marriage ceremony between Dr. Nnaemeka and I was a memorable event.

I wanted all aspect of my culture to be observed as I wanted to respect my family, my people, who were very good and kind to me.

There are pre- traditional wedding activities which must happen before the big event (ibu nmayi ukwu). None of the events will happen on Nkwo market day or Afo ukwu. In my culture and in many other Igbo lands, there are four market days - Nkwo, Eke, Orie and Afo. It is not clear to me why my people choose Nkwo as their market day but legend has it that the other neighboring towns have their market days on different days, such as Ututu Market is on Afo, Ihechiowa market is on Orie, Isu's market is on Eke, while Arochukwu's market day remain on Nkwo. These market days were distributed so that they will not happen on the same day. Alternate Afo is Afo ukwu. Afo ukwu was and still is considered to be a sacred day in my town — as it was a tradition handed over by our forefathers. No traditional marriage ceremony can take place on Nkwo nor Afo Ukwu market days.

Nnaemeka's family came from a different town in Imo State and my paternal uncle liaised with his uncles and a list of activities as well as the related items that his family was expected to bring.

The activities included the pre-wedding event of the Nnaemeka's family visiting my family, for knocking at the door (ikutu aka), which involves asking questions and finding out the availability of the girl and confirming her readiness and preparedness to move forward with the traditional marriage.

Once this is done, the "Ihe ahuru na ulo" tradition will be done, same day or another day.

After the approval to move forward by the girl's family, a list of marriage rites and requirements are then provided to the man's family. When the man's family is ready, a date is provided to them and if an agreement is reached the date of "ibu nmayi ukwu" is scheduled, which involves payment of bride price and dropping of big pads of "aju" for carrying the main wine for use in the traditional wedding.

This ceremony in the Arochukwu town is always elaborate. The Aros are normally perceived as a very proud, highly educated and well-placed community among their neighbors.

Nnaemeka's family was very prepared; they brought more than enough to make everyone joyful.

My favorite and unforgettable moment of the day was the Odu Mgbede dance, a popular dance steps popularized after the War. Prior to this time, the Aro young girl dance or bride dance was Ojojo, a graceful dance movement of the bride with her friends and sometimes family. This beautiful traditional Ojojo dance was fast taken over by the Odu Mgbede dance movement popularized by my Atani village.

Many people of Arochukwu origin, who came back from the almost two hundred and fifty (250) Arochukwu communities after the war, came back and infused the dance movements of the Ikwerre and the Owerri dance culture. They were faster, depicting well-choreographed waist movements and leg coordination. It boosted the popular Odu Mgbede dance in Arochukwu.

The church wedding took place at the St. Andrews Presbyterian Church of Nigerian, Uwani Enugu. We made our residence in Enugu.

A few months later, our daughter, Chidinma (God is good) was born; and two years later, our son, Chukwuebuka (God is great) was born.

The fulfillment of a happy marriage and the gift of children made me happy and complete, but the pain of the disappearance of my first fruit remained unchanged.

Each time I remember him I will pray to God to keep, protect and to make it possible for us to meet.

After five years, my husband got a job in Lagos with one of the big hospitals as a specialist Surgeon.

As a nurse, I decided to use the opportunity to upgrade my nursing skills, hence I sought and obtained admission at the University of Lagos for my Master's degree in nursing. It was in this institution that I met Prof. Grace Ishaku. Coincidentally, she was from Langtan. I developed a relationship with her over time and one day I asked if she knew the Banfa family. She said, "Yes" Then I inquired if she knew James Banfa. She looked at me and said, "Of course, yes, he is my cousin but has been deceased since during the war."

She wanted to know how a younger person like me knew James, I immediately lied and told her "he was an older cousin's mate in the army and my cousin had mentioned that both were friends." I asked, "What about his son?" She said that he never had any children and his parents passed a few years ago and she attended the burial of both of them.

It was a sad day for me as I immediately knew that my baby was stolen and gone, never coming back to me, or to the father's family.

Before I left Enugu, I stayed in touch with aunty Idong who assisted me after I ran away from the war camp in Ikot Effiong to

Ikoro Abasi.

I had written to her to tell about the movement of my family from Enugu to Lagos and had sent another letter to her after I arrived Lagos, providing her with my phone number and address in Lagos. One Saturday morning she called me and told me that an investigator had gone to the former war camp area asking questions of a young Igbo War Victim girl whose baby was stolen many years back. He was directed to her sister's family and he had dropped his card with one of the young men, who gave the card to her sister, Mrs. Nkoyo Akpan. She kept the card hidden properly until when her sister, Idong visited recently, she gave Idong the card.

I could not believe my eyes and I asked for the contact details of the investigator, and Aunty Idong gave me the details. The card had both Lagos as well as Abuja telephone numbers.

On Monday morning, I opted to skip my classes that day but rather to stay and get in contact with this investigator. I called the Lagos number. I first spoke with a secretary who connected me to a husky voice, well-spoken man. When I mentioned my name and the reason for my call, I could tell the excitement from his voice, when he asked me if I have information regarding his quest. Not knowing who he was and why he was looking for the victim Igbo girl, I said I might have information about the lady he was looking for. When I probed to know why he was looking for her, he said he will only speak more when he meets me face to face.

We scheduled an appointment to meet on Friday as he will be away from Lagos until Thursday. The next few days was one of the longest days of my life. I had discussed this with my husband who encouraged me that it is a good development and that he believes that more solutions will come from that meeting. On second thought, he opted to go with me to support me as he noticed that it will be too much for me, especially if the news is not positive.

When we got to the investigator's office that fateful Friday, we were directed to the conference room by the lady at the reception desk. She offered tea, coffee, and water and we gladly accepted to drink tea. Tea was eventually served to us. After some minutes a stocky, pot-bellied and well-dressed man emerged from the corridor, introduced himself as Inspector Bankole.

He asked, "Are you the lady I spoke with?" I responded in the affirmative. I was smartly dressed in blue pant suits that made me look ten years younger than my actual age. I introduced myself as Mrs. Mercy Nnaemeka and my husband introduced himself. Inspector Bankole asked, "Who are you and why are you looking for a young girl, who was a victim during the war at the Ikot-Effiong Military Camp, whose son was stolen from her as a baby?"

He immediately said, "I am looking for her because that her baby survived the war. He is alive and looking for his mother. I jumped up from my seat and asked, "Where's he; please tell me, where is he?"

Inspector Bankole looked at me not him and said that he can only speak to the mother of the baby, if she is still alive. My husband responded, "Yes, she is still alive." My husband at this time asked him to tell us the story of his client. He said his client will like to tell his own story himself, but he is not in the country right now.

My husband continued by saying that "the only way we can know if your client is the right person is when we hear his story, know what he knows so that we can compare notes with him to figure out if he is the right person or the wrong person." Bankole agreed with us but insisted that the mother of the man must come, and we insisted that the man himself must come.

Every effort to get him to answer other questions was abortive. My husband dropped his card with him and asked him to contact him when he has more information.

Inspector Bankole wanted to know our relationship with the mother, we just told him that she is our sister. Not knowing what to believe as there are many fraudulent schemes these days, my husband and I came out of that office worried.

I was devastated and infuriated, that the memory of the full episode rushed back to me. It is now the year 2000. In the past thirty-two (32) years, I have lived a life of hope, in order to ease the injustice of kidnaping, murder, rape, theft, child molestation, and even genocide committed against the Igbo and other Biafrans/Easterners. The agonies of the war remains strong rooted in the hearts of the oppressed many years after the war had ended and sometimes forever. Wounded soldiers always will say that the initial sensation of being hit by a missile is like being struck with a stone or a lump of mud, but the pain lingers, eventually heals and most times remain as scars. The scars remain as reminders of the physical wound they had, but with psychological war pains of both combat and the non-combat individuals, the victim of different kinds of atrocities end up with inner wounds that remain with them and keep them permanently and psychologically traumatized, until the inner scars are addressed.

I stayed in touch with inspector Bankole, asking for updates and each time he will say that he will let me know if he had any information from his client. His indifference was worrisome, annoying and demoralizing.

9
MEETING
MY SON

On this September day, Nnaemeka came back from work excited that the Nigerian Medical Association was hosting the new Minister of Health and that he and some of his colleagues were invited to the occasion. Since it was an evening affair, they can bring their spouses. I accepted to attend the event with him.

On getting to the venue of the event that day which took place at the multipurpose civic auditorium, located in the heart of Lagos Island. It is called the MUSON Centre (Musical Society of Nigeria). It is one of the edifices that our country can be proud of. The hall was well decorated and there were many Medical professional colleagues of my husband, whom we had met in various functions. We were directed to look for our names and table at the outer hall while we were having "Hors d'oeuvres" and greeting friends and colleagues.

On our table there were four other couples and later the fifth couple joined us. The seats and names of each couple were neatly placed on each table. I was busy discussing with the lady on my right side when I noticed that a couple who just sat down were talking to my husband. I turned to hear them introducing themselves and my husband reciprocated by introducing us.

I could not believe my eyes when I saw an exact replica of Captain James Banfa. I asked again for his name. He said: Dr. Dahiru Hamza and the lady is my fiancee, Dr. Obianuju Okorafor. They live in England and had just come to visit family and friends at home. The new Minister of Health is an old family friend; hence they came to join others in honoring him. Throughout the evening, I kept looking at him and from the corner of my eye I could see that he was also watching me intermittently. When it was the turn of our table to get our food, the ladies went first, I gravitated towards his fiancée and we talked as we went, while we walked and talked, I noticed that her fiancé, Dr Dahiru talked with my husband. He was very friendly and intelligent.

I asked her how they met, and she mentioned that they met in England. I inquisitively asked, "Are you both Christians?"

She laughed and said no and continued, "He is from a Muslim family while I come from a Christian family. I do not think it matters because he is a good man and we will make it work."

We came back to our seats to eat and talk some more. It was a good evening. When the music session started, I danced with my husband and to change partners I encouraged my husband to dance with Dr. Obianuju, while her fiancé, Dr. Dahiru came over to me.

As we danced along, I asked him if he is "related to one James Banfa."

He asked me "why." I told him that "You look exactly like him. He is someone I used to know many years back."

He said he would want to meet this person that looks like him. I told him that it is not possible as he died many years ago during the civil war. He said to me, for you to still remember how he looked, he must be someone very dear to you.

I said "Yes, he was, an officer and a gentleman. He was a good and kind man, who saved my life during the civil war."

Dr. Dahiru said, "I am so happy to hear this. This is good news to me, to hear that my late father was a good man."

I stopped dancing, looked at him and inquisitively yelled "Father?"

"Yes, he was my father."

"I did not know he was married" I quipped.

"I am not sure if he was but, I strongly believe that I am that baby boy you have been looking for", he said with a smile on his face. "What do you mean", I asked, inquisitively?

"I am not sure what my name was at birth, but I believe I was a product of Captain James Banfa, the man I look like and a beautiful Igbo mother, like you."

My feet could no longer hold me, I fell into his arms and I held him as I was holding a baby. I yelled "Baby James, Onyekachi, is this you?" I shouted. While I was shouting no one could hear me as King Sunny Ade song titled Merciful God & Baba Moke Pe O was blasting in the hall. Dr. Dahiru, suddenly said, you look much younger than I have imagined.

At this point, my joy knew no bounds, holding and talking to my son, after 32 years he was stolen from me. He was emotional too, but he asked me to control myself as his fiancée is not aware of what was going on. I asked him, if I could run and tell my husband now, he advised against it, and advised for us to meet tomorrow for lunch. Dr Dahiru gave me his card and asked me to call him. He also said that I can bring my husband. He begged me to control myself, that it will be better to take this off this venue. He did not want to answer any questions but advised that tomorrow will be a better day to discuss. The emotion was intense hence I opted to visit the ladies' room, while he went back to the seat. On getting back to the table it was awkward, but I know that my husband noticed a change in my disposition, but according to him, he thought I was enjoying the moment.

When it was time to say goodbye, my son indicated to my husband that he would want to meet us again. Nnaemeka also acknowledged the same and they exchanged contact information. Once we were alone in the car, I narrated to Nnaemeka what transpired during the dance and he was initially shocked, but was happy for me, knowing that my wish of one day seeing my boy has come through, not only seeing him but dancing and talking with him. How did he find us? I asked and how did they end up seating next to us at the table. Nnaemeka said that we will find out eventually when we finally meet with him tomorrow.

10
CONNECTING
THE DOTS

By the time I called him the next day, he was already waiting for my call. At his request, we met at the Chinese restaurant in Ikoyi.

Nnaemeka decided that it was best I go alone, so that we will be free to exchange information.

Nnaemeka was right. It was a happy meeting, but on noticing that I was alone, he requested for us to stay at the back garden. I needed to hear his story first. He heaved a sigh of relief, stretched his back, turned his neck and looked directly at me with tears of joy in his eyes.

He started by saying "I had an extremely happy childhood. My life was perfect until I came home for my mother's funeral and I was given a tell-all letter she saved for me when she died of cancer and my father's confirmation of the truths....

I wanted to hurt myself, I blamed myself, and finally estranged from my proud heritage, which I have known all my life. It resulted in my almost getting out of my medical housemanship and residency program.

One day I counseled myself and decided to speak with a therapist, whom I felt was ideal to guide me through the process of healing. It was strenuous to commence the disclosure of the facts surrounding my situation but disclosing and discussing it assisted me in unleashing my feelings about it and helped me to look for my roots. After wallowing in shelf pity for a long time I realized that life is just like that. People get ill, people get well; families grow and shrink; fortunes and futures can change with the click of a computer mouse. It was difficult but I gave myself time to adjust to the situation.

I decided not to allow the painful hurt that I felt, the resentment of my father, the anger and hatred I felt, take away space in my head, as it represents slow debilitating energy that takes away my joy and control of myself. I finally released them, decided to forgive my father as he has been requesting for months.

I called him, he was surprised and happy to hear from me, and he told me he was coming to England for medical treatment with one of his younger wives. I met up with him many times and we talked and he begged for forgiveness which I confirmed that I have already forgiven him and he encouraged me to look for my birth mother and that he will tell the truth and was ready to be punished for his mistakes. That was when I commenced the initiative to look for you.

The information he provided made it possible to find you as he also has started way before me to look for you. He passed away last year, and he had asked me to plead with you to forgive him and his wife for their selfish actions. He asked me to give you this letter on his death bed. Please find it in your heart to forgive them. He handed the letter to me, but I did not read it, as I was more interested in his story. As a functional adult now, he said, he has managed to put this trauma behind him. His father did not disclose this to anyone else. He left it up to him to decide on what to do and left him lots of his properties and resources as his first son.

My son also confided in me that he has found a woman who he believes is made for him and that he will be getting married in a few months now to a wonderful woman that he loves and would like to begin his home without any baggage. She is from a town called Ovim in Abia State.

I told him that Dr Obianuju's town is only an hour to Arochukwu. He was delighted that and he confirmed that he already knows, but the lady does not have a clue that he has an Igbo blood in his veins. I was grateful that "my God has perfected my life in his own way, placing all the lines pleasant places."

As he was talking, I realized that there are other remaining things we needed to do, to be sure. I quickly asked, how he knew I was the mother, he has been looking for him, he smiled and confirmed that his father had hired Mr. Bankole and had sent people to go and conduct investigations at Ikot-Effiong.

I also said it would be better to do a DNA test to confirm but he quickly responded that it has been done already. I asked how and when? He smiled again and confirmed that the DNA samples were collected during our meeting with the investigator, Mr. Bankole. He confirmed that Inspector Mr. Bankole was a retired Military intelligence officer, who later read law and became an investigator and a lawyer. We suspected that if you and your husband are related to me, as you stated when you met with him, that the DNA will confirm it. The sample results of the DNA obtained from you indicated that you are not only related to me, but you are actually my biological mother. Your meeting with him was videotaped and when I saw the results and the video, I could not believe that such a young, beautiful, petite woman could bear a son as tall and as old as me.

By the time he finished his story I rushed out of my seat to his arms to hug him. We both cried and hugged each other and was unable to eat the rest of the food that was brought. He listened patiently as I told him the story of my life, losing my parents at an early age, being kidnaped from the "udara tree" in my village and my journey to the war camp in Ikot Effiong, my relationship with Captain James Banfa, his birth father and the painful saga of my Baby James being snatched away from me....

Remarkably, as I was looking for him, he found me; as he was looking for me, I found him.

Lesson: The fateful journeys of our lives and the abiding lesson that a treasure will always be found, at the right time....

www.ingramcontent.com/pod-product-compliance
Lightning Source LLC
Chambersburg PA
CBHW030534020726
47494CB00004B/1360